I0583790

CHESS
MOVES

CHESS MOVES

A YA Coming-of-Age Short

MICHAEL WALKER-THOMAS

© Michael Walker-Thomas

All Rights Reserved.

No part of this publication in print or in electronic format may be reproduced, stored in a retrieval system, or transmitted in any form or by any means, electronic, mechanical, photocopying, recording, or otherwise without the prior written permission of the publisher.

This is a work of fiction. Names, characters, organizations, places, events and incidents are either the products of the author's imagination or are used fictitiously. Any resemblance to actual persons, living or dead, or actual events is purely coincidental.

Cover Art by Amy Wolbach

ISBN: 978-1-64704-181-6 (paperback)
ISBN: 978-1-64704-182-3 (eBook)

CONTENTS

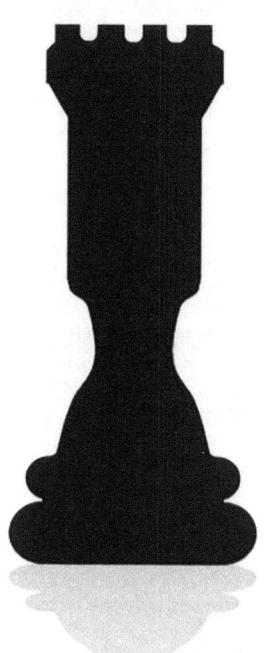

CHAPTER 1

THE OVERVIEW

t was on his mind most of the time, a time when most will go left or right. Young Lamont Barker will have to make that decision. Lamont is an 18 year old senior, and in the fall he will be attending college, "Which one shall I choose" says Lamont to himself. Lamont has a group of friends consisting of the cool crowd and the "smart crowd". In life we all have to make big decisions, this story is Lamont's.

When Lamont was younger, he would always compete, whether it was in sports, game shows or racing with his father. Lamont grew up with his two parents, but no siblings, so he leaned on making new friends or just hanging with Mom and Dad.

"Hey Lamont remember in fourth grade when you had to decide which club you wanted to be in?" his Mom said.

"Yes Mom, but this is college. This is the biggest decision of my life." Lamont says. As Lamont's Dad walks in, Lamont starts to huff and puff. "Mom, Dad, you two don't get it. There is a lot of pressure on me. Half of my friends are going to Prep University and the other half are going to State University." Lamont says.

"Well son, I can tell you one thing, me and your mother did not go to college, but we worked so hard for you. It is a blessing that you even have this decision to make." his Dad says.

"Dad, I love Prep and I love State, but Prep is the top school in the country and that would be a great opportunity for me." Lamont says. Lamont has been a straight A student since he was young. He never received anything lower than an A. "At state I can keep playing chess and also get into a great Doctoral program." Lamont says. Lamont's dream is to be a medical doctor, like the ones he sees on TV. "Chicago Med, The Good Doctor, Grey's Anatomy, I just want to be like them but better." Lamont says.

Prep University is the number one school in the country. Prestige doctors, lawyers and many political figures have gone there. Lamont got in to Prep and he is ready. Prep is known for its tough classes, but you also have to get almost a perfect on your SAT. Lamont got a perfect on his SAT and Prep accepted him. The only problem with Prep is that it is considered the "nerd school" to his friends. Only three of Lamont's friends are going there. The other seven of his friends are all going to State University.

State is a good school, but it's no Prep. State is a school most get into and it is considered the party school. Lamont knows he has a big decision to make. Should he go to State and be like most of his friends, or should he go to Prep, be looked at like he is perfect, but also receive the best education in the world. This is Lamont's decision, this is about Chess Moves, this is his life.

Welcome to Chess Moves.

CHAPTER 2

THE STATE UNIVERSITY

Today is just another day at school. Lamont goes to class, does his work and hangs with friends.

"Hey Lamont, you make a decision yet?" his friend says.

"No not yet, the deadline is in two days I know." Lamont says.

"Yeah man, you know we are waiting for you at State". his friends say.

"You mean Prep!". His three friends say out loud. "Man, Prep is for nerds, if you go there then you are not going to have fun, and you will just be studying all day dude" his friend says. "I like state, they also have a doctoral program. Don't get me wrong, I would love to go there, but I have to do what is best for me." Lamont says. When the day is over Lamont is going to study, watch some TV and then head to the baseball game at school with his dad. "Hey Lamont, Prep or State" a student asked. "To be honest I don't even know yet. I will let everyone know Friday. On this Wednesday Lamont's mind is cluttered. Lamont has been at the top of his class for four years now in high school. Everyone sees him working hard every day and doing what he is supposed to be doing. Lamont sometimes wonders about getting out of his shell and getting out of his comfort zone. All his life Lamont has been tapped inside of his work and getting the best grades. State University is considered the cool school. That is the school where Lamont can get outside of his comfort zone, find himself and become a new person. State is where Lamont will join most of his friends, but also make new friends. State might be the choice. "If I go to state, then I will become cool, I will become someone I don't even know yet, that might be my next move" Lamont says. "But it has to be like Chess Lamont, it has to be. Before you make that move, consider the move after that also" his Dad says. Lamont loves Chess, his Dad taught him how to play. Lamont's favorite piece is the Rook. Rooks can go left and right, and up and down. The reason he loves the rook is because it relates to life. You can go left or right, and you can also go up or down. Life is all about the choices and moves you make. Like Chess, your next move will either win you the game or lose you the game. If Lamont chooses State University then he may think it is the right decision, but who knows. State may or may not be the right choice.

CHAPTER 3

THE PREP UNIVERSITY

"Hey Lamont, to be honest you have to choose Prep. We will have so much fun" his friend says. "I know, but what if I get there and I just stay the same person, what if I am not happy." says Lamont. "Look, in life there are a lot of what ifs. You just have to make the right choice for yourself." his friend says. "Prep is the best school I know" Lamont says sarcastically. Prep University has so many pros and little cons. Prep will give Lamont the chance of a lifetime to do what he has always wanted to do, which is become a great doctor. "That is the goal, become the best doctor and then take care of people for a living" Lamont says. "Honestly, I just love giving back and treating people. I feel like Prep will be that, so yeah maybe I will go with you three. I got options but I do love prep" Lamont says. Lamont always had the most confidence in school, ever since he was younger, he wanted to accomplish great things in life. Going to Prep, a school not just anyone can get into, will be a dream come true for Lamont. Prep is the type of school that you go to if accepted. Lamont understands that, he knows. "So Lamont, how was your day". His Mom says. "My day was cool, studying hard and now I am going to do some last second research on these schools, I will start with Prep." Lamont says. Prep University doctors are all over the world, many in England, The United States and other places. The top doctors come out of Prep University with skill and great knowledge. "The best thing I would love about being a Doctor is the fact I can take care of someone and help. I care for people so much

Mom, I just want to give back and do something I love every day" Lamont says. "I think you will know your decision by Friday. The best thing you can do tonight is relax and then sit down with us tomorrow and we can help, but this has to be your decision. Me and your father do not want to interfere." his Mom says. "Yes I know Mom. Thank you. I am looking at Prep stuff now before I relax." Lamont says.

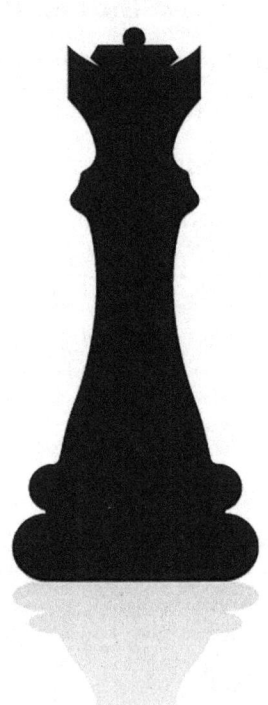

CHAPTER 4

THE FAMILY

The Cool school or the Not cool school, that is the question. That weighs on Lamont every day. Lamont's favorite quote is by W.E.B Du Bois. "Education must simply not teach work, it must teach life". Lamont Barker always wonders about that quote and how it could go two ways. By understanding that education must not only teach work can go into his State University decision. At Prep it will be all about work and not so much living socially with his friends. It will teach him about life and it will also teach him about school. At Prep though, he looks at the quote differently. Prep University is also teaching him about life, life after school. He wants to become a doctor. Lamont knows his social life may not be that great, but for the rest of his life he will become what he has always wanted to become. "Maybe I can party, do my school work and make new friends. State might be the best experience I ever had" Lamont ponders. "OK Lamont now let's all discuss as a family about what you are going to do tomorrow." His Mom says. "Dad, Mom, as I sat down last night and thought about it, I really want to go to State University, but I really want to go to Prep." Lamont says. "Prep is not home son, Prep is about a 16 hour drive from home. Lamont this has to be your call. State is your home school." His Dad says. "Lamont, we know you want to be a doctor and that is great, but don't you also want to experience college and get out of your comfort zone" his Mom says. "Yes Mom, Yes Dad, you two are right. I believe I will make the right decision for me. One thing I love is that you two are right by my side with whatever decision I make. That is all I could ever ask for is support." Lamont says.

Prep University or State University? Lamont ponders, walks back and forth and carries on the conversation with his parents. In the morning, the biggest decision of his life will have to be made. "What will my friends think about me? Will I become uncool or will I become this party guy that I never have been before." Lamont Ponders. Those are some of the questions he will have to address to his friends, but for now it is over with his parents. He has told them tonight, but tomorrow he will have to tell his friends, teachers and school. Lamont Barker, straight A student and the top of his class. This Chess Move will be made loud, unlike Chess, but he is happy with his decision, staring at the wall and it is silent, like a game of Chess.

CHAPTER 5

THE DECISION

After telling his parents, Lamont wakes up to text messages and phone calls from his friends. He will not tell them until he sees them this morning in school. It is decision day, and Lamont is ready to face the world. Lamont goes to his first class of the day, his only class without any of his friends. The teacher asks everyone write down one thing they want to do next year in college that will build their legacy. "Next year I want to stay focused and become great. The school I chose last night will give me the best opportunity to be myself, be great, and build my legacy. I know if I work hard at school and building myself, then I will succeed. This journey has been long and stressful, but my life starts now. 12th grade has been fun, I love my friends and family, but this is my time." Lamont writes. "Class turn in your papers, you can take a picture of what you wrote. Maybe also you can hang it up on your dorm wall if you are going to college, if not just look at it from time to time" the teacher says. Lamont leaves class and enters the bathroom, looking at himself in the mirror before his next class. "Man, look at you. Ups and downs with yourself. I have been trying to find out who you are for the longest. When I see you I see the blessing God has given me, but I also see the future blessings. Today everyone will see me for who I am, tomorrow I am a new man." Lamont says staring at the mirror at himself. "Hey Lamont! Today is the big day, let's hear it man. Where are you going" his friends say. "I chose the best school for me, one that will take me to where I want to go in life, and one that will grow me as a person." Lamont says. "I started thinking about Prep University and I got so many great vibes from the school. I can really grow there and mature as a man. They will give me the best pathway towards being the best Doctor I can be. Then I started thinking about State University. Most of y'all are going there, and it is a great school too. I also can come out of my shell and become more of someone I don't know yet, and that's exciting. State and Prep." Lamont ponders......... "Well Lamont, which one is it?" his friends ask. I sat with my parents last night and they loved my decision. I love you all and we are still gonna text and call hopefully but next year I just want to be myself and do everything I can to be the best version of myself I can be. Next year I will be going to PREP UNIVERSITY." Lamont shouts. "Yayyyyyyy" his friends say. "Lamont, at the end of the day Prep is the best school for you. We are gonna have fun and get our study on!" His friends say. "I know you guys also wanted me to go to State, but I just want to continue to do my thing and also become the best Doctor. I know Prep will grow me as a person and as a student." Lamont says. Sometimes in life heavy decisions are everything. They can make or break you. In Chess, you have to make each move with the thought of your next move. You cannot just move without thinking about the future. In life, you have to move strategic, each day you have

to make choices. We have one life to live, just one. Make this your best life, make your next move life changing. And if you don't have any moves to make, remember, tomorrow is not promised.

Chess Moves

www.ingramcontent.com/pod-product-compliance
Lightning Source LLC
Chambersburg PA
CBHW050159110726
47898CB00008B/2868